The Wrong Side

written by
William A. Guiffré

illustrated by
Cheri Ann Baron

Coastal Publishing, Inc.
504 Amberjack Way
Summerville, SC 29485
1-843-821-6168
coastalpublishing@earthlink.net

Publisher's Cataloging-in Publication Data

William A. Guiffré
The wrong side of the bed / by William A. Guiffré ; illustrated
by Cheri Ann Baron.
p. cm.

SUMMARY: George knows it's going to be a bad day when
he gets up on the wrong side of the bed, but all is not lost when
he gets up from his nap!
Audience: Grades K-6
ISBN 1-931650-20-9 - HB
ISBN 1-931650-34-9 - PB

1. Emotions in children--Juvenile fiction. 2. Naps
(Sleep)--Juvenile fiction. [1. Emotions--Fiction.
2. Behavior--Fiction. 3. Naps (Sleep)--Fiction.
4. Stories in rhyme.] I. Baron, Cheri Ann. II. Title.

PZ8.3.G9475Wr 2002   [E]
                     QBI33-1017

In the Wrong Side of the Bed, Dr. Guiffre makes good use of repetition and exaggeration to humorously describe an experience that most children have had. Therefore, they can easily understand and sympathize with George. The illustrations not only enhance the story line but they also can become teaching tools for comprehension and vocabulary development. The Wrong Side of the Bed and Mr. Guiffre's previous book, Gramma's Glasses are fun stories for use in the classroom as well as the home.

Barbara J. Kidd, Curriculum Coordinator K-12 Potsdam Central School District, NY; Federal Programs Coordinator, Troy City Schools District NY

The Wrong Side of the Bed by William Guiffre is a delightful story that young and old can relate to. My grandchildren have read the book so many times they can now read the story almost without looking! It's a great beginning reader.

Barbara Quinn-Anderson, third grade teacher for 17 years at Wesleyan School, Atlanta Georgia.

Rhyming books are my favorites. I particularly liked this book because of the simplicity of the text and the power of the message. I will be purchasing this one for my granddaughter (kindergarten) who is just starting to read. George reminds me of several children I know. Thank you for your wonderful storytelling.

Vaughn Gagne, Librarian, Wilton Free Library Wilton. Maine.

Wake with a smile
and the Sun will always
Shine.
William A. Guiffre
March, 2015

Dr William Guiffré
Author

Following graduation from the University of Rochester, Dr William Guiffré served in the U.S. Navy for three years and returned to Upstate New York where he became an English teacher at Brighton Junior High School.

In addition to teaching, his career in public education included ten years as a guidance counselor and nineteen as an administrator, the last fifteen of which he served as high school principal in Victor, New York. After one year of retirement, he returned to serve for six years on the Victor Board of Education.

Dr. Guiffré resides with his wife Ann on Kiawah Island, South Carolina but returns to summer in Inlet, New York in the Adirondack Mountains where they can be closer to their seven children and their twenty-three grandchildren who have been the inspiration for him to write picture books for children.

Dedication - To our twenty-three grandchildren, but especially to George who inspired this story.

Foreword - You know it is going to be a bad day when George gets up on the wrong side of the bed.

Illustrator - Cheri Baron first worked as an artist in her hometown of Leominster, Massachusetts. Her parents encouraged her talent with studio art classes, and plenty of paper and paints. She attended Salem State College and became an art teacher. Newly married she moved to Milwaukee, Wisconsin where she did a series of watercolor paintings. Now Cheri's home is the Hudson River Valley in New York. Her husband Danny is a New York City firefighter. She keeps busy homeschooling their children, Alyssa and Kelsey. Cheri enjoys hiking and camping with her family. She believes that each moment they have together is a gift, and she is grateful for it.

In the morn, when George wakes up

In the early pre-dawn hour,

If, from the wrong side of the bed he goes,

His whole day will be sour.

With folded arms across his chest

And thunder scowl on face,

He starts his list of "I don't likes"

And stomps his foot in place.

"I don't like this. I don't like that.
I don't like thin and I don't like fat.

I don't like hot. I don't like cold.

I don't like young and I don't like old."

"I don't like books. I don't like toys.

I don't like girls and I don't like boys.

I don't like shopping. I don't like schools.

I don't like living by the rules."

"I don't like cats. I don't like dogs.

I don't like snakes and I don't like frogs.

I don't like wet. I don't like dry.
I don't like fish or birds that fly."

"I don't like up. I don't like down.

I don't like smiles or clowns that frown.

I don't like dark. I don't like light.

I don't like noises in the night."

"I don't like cookies. I don't like roasts

I don't like tuna and I don't like toast.

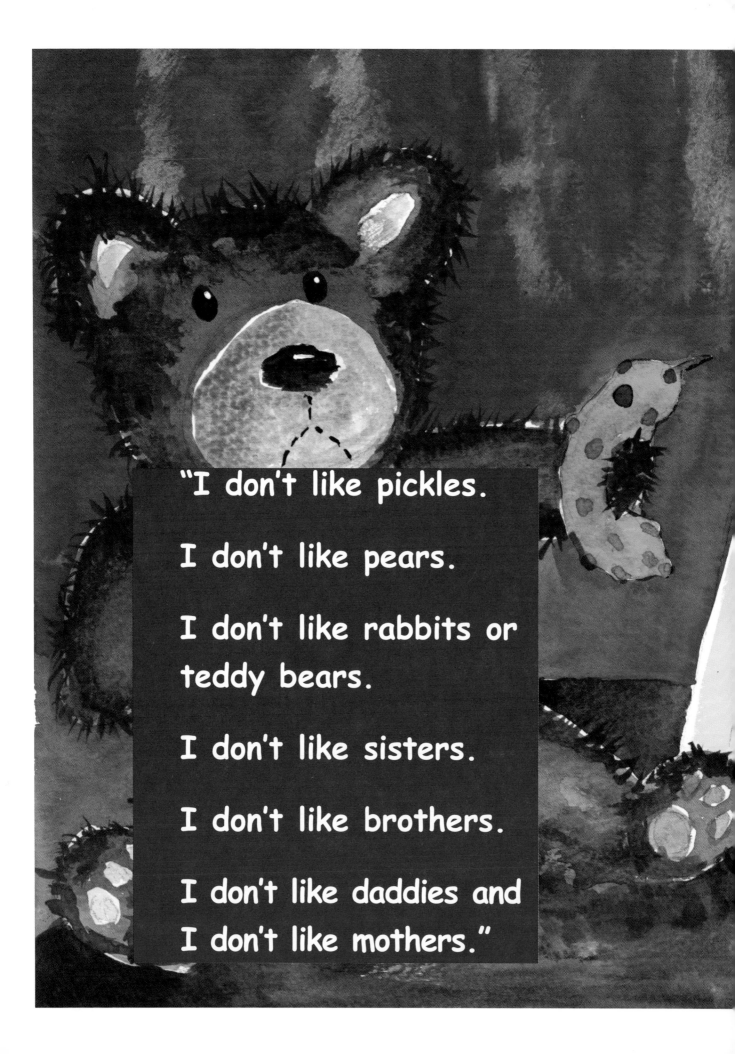

"I don't like pickles.

I don't like pears.

I don't like rabbits or teddy bears.

I don't like sisters.

I don't like brothers.

I don't like daddies and I don't like mothers."

The "I don't likes" continued
for at least another hour,

But no one even listened and
Mom just took a shower.

"Okay, George, now that
will do!

Your list of "I don't likes"
is through.

Go right upstairs and get in
bed.

You need some time to clear
your head.

When you get up, let it be
said.

You chose the other side of
bed."

His nap was over and down he came,

But little George was not the same.

The thunder scowl had left his face.

Instead there was a smile in place.

"I do like this. I do like that.

I do like thin and I do like fat.

I do like hot. I do like cold.

I do like young and I do like old."

"I do like books. I do like toys.

I do like girls and I do like boys.

I do like shopping. I do like schools.

I'll go on living by the rules."

" I do like cats. I do like dogs.

I do like snakes and I do like frogs.

I do like wet. I do like dry.

I do like fish and birds that fly."

"I do like up. I do like down.

I do like smiles and clowns that frown.

I do like dark. I do like light.

And even noises in the night."

"I do like up. I do like down.

"I do like cookies. I do like roasts.

I do like tuna and I do like toast.

I do like spinach. I do like peas.

I do like Thank You and I do like Please."

"I do like pickles. I do like pears.

I do like rabbits and teddy bears.

I do like sisters.

I do like brothers.

I do like daddies and
I do like mothers."

Now George's lists
are finally through.

It's time to know
that George likes you!